FAMOUS IMMIGRANT
POLITICIANS

MAKING AMERICA GREAT
IMMIGRANT SUCCESS STORIES

FAMOUS IMMIGRANT
POLITICIANS

Susan Nichols

Enslow Publishing

101 W. 23rd Street
Suite 240
New York, NY 10011
USA

enslow.com

Published in 2018 by Enslow Publishing, LLC.
101 W. 23rd Street, Suite 240, New York, NY 10011

Library of Congress Cataloging-in-Publication Data

Names: Nichols, Susan, 1975–author.
Title: Famous immigrant politicians / by Susan Nichols.
Description: New York : Enslow Publishing, [2018] | Series: Making America
great : immigrant success stories | Includes bibliographical references
and index. | Audience: Grades: 7–12.
Identifiers: LCCN 2017015084 | ISBN 9780766092426 (library bound) | ISBN 9780766095885
(paperback)
Subjects: LCSH: Immigrants—Political activity—United States—Juvenile
literature. | Immigrants—United States—Biography—Juvenile literature. |
Politicians—United States—Biography—Juvenile literature.
Classification: LCC E184.A1 N495 2018 | DDC 305.9/06912073—dc23
LC record available at https://lccn.loc.gov/2017015084

Printed in the United States of America

To Our Readers: We have done our best to make sure all websites in this book were active and appropriate when we went to press. However, the author and the publisher have no control over and assume no liability for the material available on those websites or on any websites they may link to. Any comments or suggestions can be sent by email to customerservice@enslow.com.

Photo credits: Cover, pp. 3, 36–37, 94–95 Tom Williams/CQ Roll Call Group/Getty Images; pp. 6–7, 14 Bettmann/Getty Images; p. 10 Stock Montage/Archive Photos/Getty Images; p. 16 Culture Club/ Hulton Archive/Getty Images; p. 18 Public Domain/loc.gov; pp. 20–21, 26–27, 28–29, 42, 44, 47, 65, 69, 72, 78–79 Library of Congress Prints and Photographs Division; pp. 22–23 Sanchai Kumar/ Shutterstock.com; pp. 32–33 Wally McNamee/Corbis Historical/Getty Images; p. 34 Cynthia Johnson/ The LIFE Images Collection/Getty Images; p. 39 Ed Clark/The LIFE Picture Collection/Getty Images; p. 49 © AP Images; pp. 50–51 Alex Wong/Getty Images; p. 53 Daniel Acker/Bloomberg/Getty Images; pp. 56–57 GraphicaArtis/Archive Photos/Getty Images; pp. 58–59 Robert Alexander/Archive Photos/ Getty Images; pp. 62–63 Universal History Archive/Getty Images; p. 67 Joe Seer/Shutterstock.com; pp. 74–75 Tony Linck/The LIFE Images Collection/Getty Images; p. 76 Joe Raedle/Getty Images; pp. 80–81 Aaron Davidson/WireImage/Getty Images; pp. 84–85 AFP/Getty Images; p. 87 Paul Connell/The Boston Globe/Getty Images; p. 90 Joyce Naltchayan/AFP/Getty Images; pp. 92–93 Chip Somodevilla/Getty Images; cover and interior pages Saicle/Shutterstock.com (flag).

Contents

Introduction

IMMIGRANTS AT THE CONSTITUTIONAL CONVENTION

On September 17, 1787, thirty-nine American men met in Philadelphia for an important task. Their actions would shape the future of the thirteen colonies that had just finished a long war against England.

Britain did not want to grant independence to its North American colonies because it made a great deal of money from them. But the Americans were sick of unfair treatment and paying high taxes to the British government, so they fought hard to win the Revolutionary War—and they did.

But what they were left with was a job possibly even more difficult than war—they had to create their own government.

What shape should that government take? The delegates from the colonies definitely knew what they didn't want in a government. For example, they agreed they didn't want a monarchy. They had just suffered for years in a drawn-out war to be free of a monarch, or a ruler.

The Americans also believed that a government should serve the interests of the people it governed. In the end, they invented a system in which the government got its rights from the people. They also made sure they would never have a monarchy by splitting the powers of the government into three separate branches: executive (the president), legislative

The members of the Constitutional Convention were a group of American men, including Benjamin Franklin, who met after the Revolutionary War to approve a system of government for the new country.

(the Congress, which includes the House of Representatives and the Senate), and judicial (the Supreme Court).

The idea of the United States was completely new, and some historians would point out that it still is. It is a functional democracy, which means that people choose their leaders, and those leaders transfer power peacefully when their terms end.

This unique form of government took off on September 17, 1787, when thirty-nine men put their names on the newly written United States Constitution. Many Americans don't know that nine of the signers were not born in the country. They were immigrants— men who had left their homes overseas to build a new life in the United States. These men moved to the colonies bent on making them their permanent home. As a result, they cared whether the colonies succeeded.

Alexander Hamilton, a representative from New York, was born in the British West Indies. His father, a Scotsman, abandoned him and his mother, a British-French woman who died when Hamilton was young. Fortunately for him, a wealthy family adopted him, and he went on to attend King's College (now Columbia University) in New York. Hamilton liked New York and decided to stay.

In addition to Hamilton, James Wilson of Pennsylvania was born in Scotland. After attending college at St. Andrews in Glasgow and Edinburgh, he moved to Philadelphia and studied law. He became involved in the Revolution and supported the independence effort.

The participation of people like Hamilton and Wilson in the drafting of the Constitution leaves little doubt that immigrants have shaped the US government for more than 250 years. Since the signing of the Constitution, hundreds of immigrants have served the political needs of the United States.

CHAPTER 1

AMERICA'S FIRST IMMIGRANT CONGRESSMEN

M any immigrants served in the United States Congress from the earliest years of our nation. This chapter will highlight some of those Americans, from the Revolutionary era through the Civil War and World War I.

WILLIAM PATERSON

William Paterson stands out as one of the most important politicians in the early days of the United States. He was born in Ireland on December 24, 1745, and immigrated to the American colonies when he was still a child. His parents moved around for a few years before eventually settling in New Jersey. His father earned a living as a merchant and made enough money to send Paterson to expensive private schools. He attended the College of New Jersey (later renamed Princeton University).

While in the colonies, he became caught up in the revolution of the colonists against England's King George. He served in the colonial military as an officer in a local militia. He became a delegate from New Jersey to the Federal Constitutional Convention in Philadelphia in 1787, where he became one of the signers of the Constitution.

William Paterson was born in Ireland, but he made his career as a senator, governor, and judge in the United States. He signed the US Constitution.

Paterson held several positions in state administration, including New Jersey attorney general. He won a seat in the United States Senate and served from March 4, 1789, to November 13, 1790. He only stepped down as senator because he'd been elected governor of New Jersey.

He resigned as governor in 1793 when he was appointed associate justice of the US Supreme Court. George Washington, the first president of the United States, appointed Paterson. For the honor, Paterson served dutifully, even though he had health problems. According to Biography.com, "In 1803, Paterson was hurt in a carriage accident. He was never the same after the incident, but he didn't let his physical problems distract him from his judicial duty."[1]

Paterson served on the Supreme Court until his death on September 9, 1806.[2]

ELIGIUS FROMENTIN

Eligius Fromentin was born in France in 1767. He grew up there, studying classic literature, language, and history, and he eventually became a Catholic priest. He worked as a priest in Etampes, France, but he would not remain there long.

The French Revolution began in 1789, and while it freed the people from the corruption of the ruling class, it also caused much unrest in the country. The Reign of Terror, or La Terreur, was a period of violence in which different political groups tried to take over. It lasted from September 1793 to July 1794. Fromentin fled his country during this time and then moved to the United States.

He settled first in Pennsylvania and then moved to Maryland, where he taught school. He also became a law student and eventually left the clergy. He moved once again to the new territory of Louisiana, where he became a successful lawyer in New Orleans. His time in the new nation of the United States was positive. He was more successful than he'd imagined he could be, and he was excited to be part of the growing country.

WAVES OF IMMIGRATION

In 1620, the Pilgrims arrived in a North America filled with Native Americans. The Pilgrims came to the United States in search of religious freedom. Later, hundreds of thousands of Africans were brought over on ships across the Atlantic and forced into slavery. According to History.com, "Although the exact numbers will never be known, it is believed that 500,000 to 650,000 Africans were brought to America and sold into slavery between the 17th and 19th centuries."

Between 1815 and 1865, a wave of immigrants came to the United States from Europe. A majority arrived from Ireland, which was experiencing a significant famine, or food shortage. Ireland is a mostly Catholic country, and the Irish often faced prejudice from anti-Catholic Americans in their new country. Also, many Americans viewed Irish immigrants as their competition for jobs because so many had come to the United States. By the 1930s, several million Irish immigrants had settled in the country.

During the 1800s, approximately five million Germans also moved to the United States, as did a large number of Chinese immigrants. Many of the Chinese newcomers hoped to strike it rich during the California gold rush, but the Chinese Exclusion Act of 1882 banned more Chinese workers from immigrating. It was the first major law that tried to stop immigrants from a certain country from entering the United States. Today, the Chinese Exclusion Act is largely viewed as racist.

As a result, Fromentin became involved in the political life of the nation. His law background helped him as he served in a number of government positions. He first was a clerk to the Orleans Territory House of Representatives from 1807 to 1811. He then served as secretary of the state senate from 1812 to 1813. Finally, he was elected to the United States Senate and served for the state of Louisiana from March 4, 1813, to March 3, 1819.

He returned to his law career after his term in office. He was appointed a federal judge for West Florida and East Florida in May 1821 but soon resigned. Fromentin returned to New Orleans and took up his private law practice again, working for a short while until his death on October 6, 1822.

ABRAHAM ALFONSE ALBERT GALLATIN

Abraham Alfonse Albert Gallatin, also known as Albert Gallatin, was born in Jan. 29, 1761, in Geneva, Switzerland. He moved to the United States at the age of nineteen and lived in Pennsylvania for a short time. He soon became involved in politics, especially with the anti-Federalists, and became known as an expert in finance.

He served in the House of Representatives from 1795 to 1801 and became a member of the newly formed House Committee on Finance, which served to oversee federal spending. The oldest committee in Congress, today it is known as the Ways and Means Committee. It is very powerful, and members are responsible for writing taxes and raising revenues, or government income. Gallatin proved to be very careful on this committee and made efforts to limit the government's spending. This made him unpopular in some circles.

Later, Gallatin served as secretary of the Treasury under President Thomas Jefferson. In the role, he "stressed simplicity in government and termination of the public debt."[5] During that time, the federal government was spending heavily to expand the navy.

Albert Gallatin, born in Switzerland, immigrated to the United States in 1780. His interest in Native American culture led him to establish the American Ethnological Society.

President Jefferson had also spent $15 million for the Louisiana Purchase in 1803. Still, as secretary of the Treasury, Gallatin found a way to lower the federal debt by $23 million over a period of eight years.[6]

The War of 1812, which broke out between the United States and the United Kingdom, troubled Gallatin. He felt certain that the war would ruin the United States and its finances. He tried to find a way to end it. In 1814, he sailed to the country of Belgium, where he negotiated a treaty, or agreement, with British representatives in the city of Ghent. The Treaty of Ghent was signed on December 24, 1814, and ended the war between the two nations. Gallatin received praise as a result.

He then served as minister to France from 1816 to 1823. He also served as minister to Great Britain from 1826 to 1827. After a while, he grew tired of political drama and retired from public service.

Settling in New York, he followed his own personal interests. He became the first president of the National Bank, which started in Manhattan in 1829. He also devoted a lot of time to studying the cultures, languages, and folklore of Native American tribes. In 1842, he founded the American Ethnological Society of New York, leading him to sometimes be referred to as the "father of American ethnology."[7]

He died Aug. 12, 1849, in the city of Astoria, New York.

PIERRE SOULÉ

Pierre Soulé was born at France's Castillon-en-Couserans, near Bordeaux, on August 31, 1801. He finished religious training at the Collège de l'Esquille at Toulouse, a Jesuit school. He was a politically active citizen of France, but many of his political views caused the government to label him a troublemaker.

As a teenager, he became involved in a plot against the Bourbons, the royal family of France. The Bourbons had returned to

Born in France, Pierre Soulé became a controversial American politician. He wrote the Ostend Manifesto in 1854, which would have extended American slavery to Cuba.

power after the French Revolution but were eventually overthrown in 1830. For his role, the fifteen-year-old Pierre was sent to Navarre, where he "worked as a shepherd boy in the Pyrennes for a year."[8] In 1818, he was pardoned, which means the government cleared his record. He continued his studies and eventually earned a law degree in Paris. He lived and practiced law in Paris, where he also published newspaper articles. He was imprisoned in 1825 for writing controversial articles that called for government changes.

Soulé escaped prison and decided to leave the country of his birth permanently. He fled to the United States, stopping first in England and then in Haiti before reaching Louisiana where he opened a law practice. But before long, he became involved in politics yet again—although this time, he enjoyed the political freedom of his new home.

Soulé was elected to the Louisiana State Senate in 1846 but soon became a member of the United States Senate. He took the seat of Senator Alexander Barrow, who had died. Soulé served from January 21, 1847, to March 3, 1847. He was again elected to serve in the Senate from March 1849 to April 1853, when he resigned from the post.

He'd found another job. President Zachary Taylor named him the American ambassador to Spain, a role in which he served from April 7, 1853, to February 1, 1855. Soulé became linked to a scandal during this period of his career. In 1854, some Southern slave-owners were trying to persuade the government that the United States should purchase Cuba, which was a slave-owning territory, from Spain. Soulé took up this issue and helped write the Ostend Manifesto, a document that spelled out this position. It suggested that the United States should consider Cuba's refusal to sell as a hostile act.

The manifesto would have led to Cuba becoming a US state. As a slave-owning state, it would have given more power to the South,

Knute Nelson, who was born in Norway, was the first Scandinavian-born American to be elected to the Senate. He fought for the Union army during the Civil War.

where residents were upset about the anti-slavery movement. Indeed, in 1861, the Civil War between the Northern and Southern states began. Abolitionists criticized Soulé for his writing, while others argued that writing the manifesto on behalf of the Southern states interfered with his role as American ambassador to Spain. According to historian J. Preston Moore, the scandal led to Soulé's "return to America under a cloud."[9]

When the Civil War broke out, Soulé supported the Confederacy, or Southern states, because he considered himself a Louisianan. In May 1861, Union soldiers captured and jailed him for treason. But, given his early years, Soulé was an expert escape artist. He did, in fact, escape prison (he'd been taken to Massachusetts) and ran back to the South. When the Confederacy surrendered in 1865, Soulé left the United States and lived in Cuba for a time.

He later returned to Louisiana, where he died on March 26, 1870.

KNUTE NELSON

Knute Nelson was the first Scandinavian American to serve in the United States Senate. He was born in Evanger, Voss, in Norway on February 2, 1843.[10] His father was not married to his mother and did not involve himself in Nelson's childhood. Knute and his mother lived in poverty on his uncle's farm until the land was sold. His uncle moved to the United States to look for work, and soon six-year-old Knute and his mother immigrated as well. They lived in Chicago for a short time with his uncle. His mother had borrowed money for the trip across the Atlantic and worked as a maid to pay off the debt. Knute worked as a paper delivery boy.

His mother eventually married another Norwegian immigrant, and they all moved to Wisconsin. He enrolled in the Albion Academy, a school the Seventh-Day Adventist Church started for low-income children. Knute studied hard and also worked part-time at the school.

Norwegian American Knute Nelson not only served in the Wisconsin State Assembly, he also represented the state of Minnesota in the US House of Representatives and later became governor there.

When Nelson turned eighteen, the Civil War broke out in his new country. He joined the military and served in the Black Hawks Rifles militia, part of the Union army. Many of his Albion schoolmates served with him, but the behavior of the militiamen disappointed them, so they transferred to the Fourth Wisconsin Volunteers. He sent a large amount of his military paycheck to his mother and stepfather. During the Battle of Port Hudson in 1863, he was shot and taken as a prisoner of war for a short period.

After the war ended, he married and settled down to build a career and start a family. He studied law in Madison, Wisconsin, and opened a successful law practice in the city of Alexandria. He worked hard on behalf of the Norwegian immigrant community, helping many of them get used to life in the United States.

LADY LIBERTY

The Statue of Liberty is an American landmark and a symbol of America's open door to immigrants and refugees. As a work of art, its actual name is "Liberty Enlightening the World." It stands on Liberty Island in New York Harbor. French sculptor Frédéric Auguste Bartholdi designed the statue, and Gustave Eiffel built it. If that name rings a bell, it's because Eiffel is the same artist who built the Eiffel Tower in Paris.

Édouard René de Laboulaye, a French abolitionist who supported the Union in the Civil War, first proposed the building of the statue. Laboulaye mentioned the idea to Bartholdi, a sculptor. They thought it would be appropriate for France to give the United States a work of art that celebrated freedom, since both nations valued independence.

Bartholdi began building parts of the statue. He built and displayed the head, for example, at the Paris World's Fair in 1878. Meanwhile, Gustave Eiffel helped with the structure. He designed the body's weight to be borne mostly by the inner framework and added two staircases, so visitors could climb to the top.

(continued on page 24)

Sculpted by Frédéric Auguste Bartholdi and dedicated in 1886, the Statue of Liberty is recognized as a symbol of freedom by people from all over the world.

(continued from page 22)

Construction work on "Lady Liberty" could not begin right away because there wasn't enough money. But then people from around the world donated money to the cause. When construction finished, the statue stood at 305 feet, from the pedestal to the torch. A dedication ceremony for the statue took place on October 28, 1886. Since then, the statue, made possible by international efforts, has greeted immigrants who come to the United States.

Between 1874 and 1895, Nelson served in a variety of political and public service positions, including Minnesota state senator, presidential elector, University of Minnesota regent, and Minnesota congressman. He was elected governor of Minnesota in 1892 and served in the role from 1893 to 1895. He stands out as the first foreign-born governor of the state.

While in office, Nelson ran for the position of United States senator and won. He represented Minnesota from March 4, 1895, to April 28, 1923. While in office, he made an important visit back to his native country of Norway, where the people received him as an honored guest. He died while in office during a train trip from Washington, DC, to Minnesota.

CHAPTER 2

IMMIGRANTS IN CONGRESS SINCE WORLD WAR I

Since World War I, many people born outside of the United States have served in both the US House of Representatives and the US Senate. This chapter will highlight some of those great Americans, beginning with Magnus Johnson, a Scandinavian who replaced the late Knute Nelson in the Senate.

MAGNUS JOHNSON

Magnus Johnson was born on September 19, 1871, in Varmland, Sweden. In Varmland, close to the Norwegian border, he attended local schools and trained to be a glassblower. In 1891, when he was twenty years old, he moved to the United States and settled in Wisconsin.

At the time, Wisconsin was one of the nation's most important lumber-producing regions. Johnson easily found work as a lumberjack for two years. In 1893, he moved to Minnesota, where he became a farmer.

In middle age, Johnson became politically active. From 1911 to 1914, he served as president of the Minnesota Union of the American Society of Equity. The organization was founded in 1902 to serve the interests of farmers and farmworkers in the United States. Many other agriculture groups modeled themselves after the

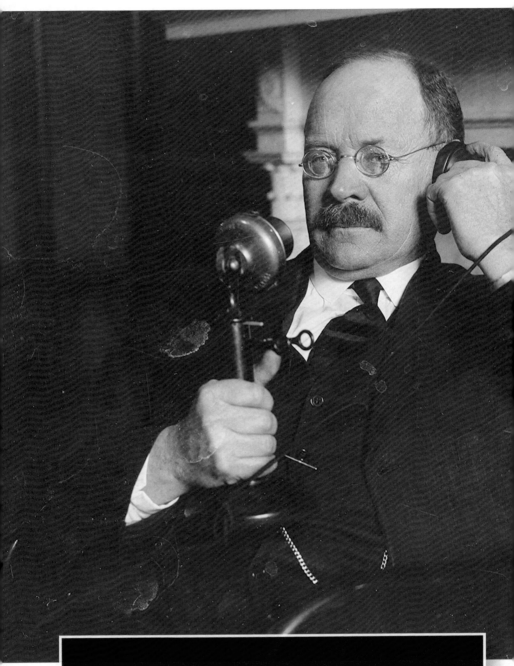

Born in Sweden, Magnus Johnson moved to Wisconsin and then to Minnesota. For many years, he worked as a lumberjack and as a farmer.

organization. A number of these groups still exist today. The American Society of Equity aimed to give agricultural workers as much power as labor union workers had. Johnson helped to organize it in its early years.

In addition, Johnson served as vice president of the Equity Cooperative Exchange from 1912 to 1926. The Exchange formed in 1908 in Minneapolis and was the "first cooperative terminal grain marketing agency of account in the United States."[1] Again, Johnson fought to give the nation's farming industry more power.

Johnson's political activism helped him win a seat in the Minnesota State House of Representatives, where he served from 1915 to 1919. To boot, he served as a member of the Minnesota Senate from 1919 to 1923. As the candidate of the Democratic Farmer-Labor Party, he ran for governor of Minnesota in 1922 and again in 1926. However, he lost both elections.

In 1923, the Minnesota Senator Knute Nelson passed away. His death led to Johnson winning the election to replace him on July 16. He served until March 3, 1925, but lost the race for reelection. He served for a time in the House of Representatives, again as a member of the Democratic Farmer-Labor Party, but lost that reelection in 1934. After serving many years in public office, Johnson returned to his agricultural work in Minnesota. He died on September 13, 1936.[2]

WISE WORDS

During World War I, when he was governor of New Mexico, Octaviano Ambrosio Larrazolo gave a powerful speech about race. People often accused him of being a "race agitator" because he stood up for ethnic and racial minorities, but Larrazolo's speech shows that he felt racial diversity could strengthen the nation.

Larrazolo said that New Mexico, which is also home to a large Native American population, proved how well different races of people could blend together as Americans. He said this achievement is a matter of pride for New Mexicans as well as a model for the nation as a whole.

"For behold, two races of people absolutely distinct from one another, different in their history, different in their traditions, different in their language, distinctions in customs, different in everything that marks the differences of the various races that compose the great family of nations," he said. "We find them side by side, with equal devotion, with equal patriotism and with equal enthusiasm, fighting for one flag, for one government, and together symbolizing one principle, the principle of Free Government!"

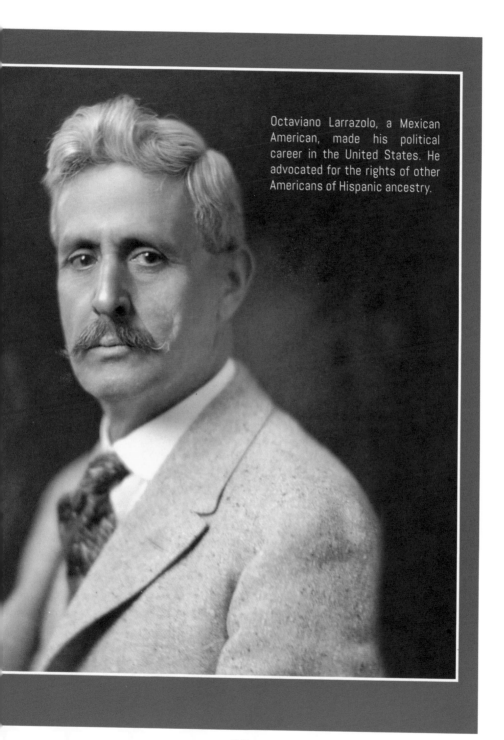

Octaviano Larrazolo, a Mexican American, made his political career in the United States. He advocated for the rights of other Americans of Hispanic ancestry.

SAM HAYAKAWA

Samuel Ichiye Hayakawa was born on July 18, 1906, in Vancouver, Canada. He attended Canadian public schools and grew up in the era of World War I. He received his undergraduate degree in 1927 from the University of Manitoba in Winnipeg, Canada. He also earned a graduate degree in English in 1928 from McGill University in Montreal. Later, he moved to the United States to attend the University of Wisconsin, Madison. There, he earned a PhD in English in 1935.

He remained in the United States, taking teaching positions at several universities, including the University of Wisconsin and the University of Chicago. In 1955, he accepted a position at San Francisco State College (now San Francisco State University). He became an expert in semantics, the field of language and logic that explores the meaning of words and phrases. Hayakawa also wrote several books that became important in the field of semantics, including *Language and Thought in Action* and *The Semantic Barrier.*

While he was a professor at San Francisco State, student riots broke out across campus. A group of students demanded that the university offer ethnic studies courses, but the university hesitated to do so. Also, the university had fired popular part-time professor George Murray because of his political views. Many faculty and students protested in peaceful ways, such as by leading strikes, but some of the protestors turned to violence. This led the university to suspend classes for several days.

It was such a rocky period that the university president, Robert Smith, resigned because of his poor management of the situation. The university named Hayakawa acting president in his place. Hayakawa had spoken out strongly against student protestors. He now had the job of getting the campus back to order.

On December 2, 1968, during his first week as acting president, Hayakawa confronted a group of protestors. He was firm in his belief that the campus must open, even if police had to be called in to restore order. He believed the university had a responsibility to teach other students who wanted to attend classes. As he tried to talk to the protestors, however, the sound of a loudspeaker on a nearby sound truck drowned him out. Determined that the students hear him, Hayakawa climbed up on the sound truck and ripped the wires out of the loudspeaker. News cameras caught him doing this and televised it live. By the next day, the English professor was famous. According to the *Washington Post*, "the slender, soft-spoken scholar with a fondness for multihued tam-o'-shanters became one of the most popular figures in California. He was dubbed 'Samurai Sam.'"[3]

In the end, despite his tough stance, Hayakawa worked with the protestors and met many of their demands, including starting an African studies program. Impressed by Hayakawa, then California Governor Ronald Reagan gave him the job of university president permanently. Hayakawa led San Francisco State for several more years. He also began writing a column for the *Register & Tribune Syndicate*.

In 1976, he ran for the United States Senate. In a surprise turn of events, Hayakawa, a newcomer to politics, defeated his opponent John V. Tunney. Many Californians viewed Hayakawa as a person who "got things done" and could bring reform to government. According to the *Los Angeles Times*, "At the time [Hayakawa] was one of the most popular public figures in the state, a hero to multitudes of Californians outraged by student militants and Vietnam War demonstrators."[4]

He served as US senator from January 2, 1977, to January 3, 1983. The media started off calling him by his nickname, "Samurai Sam." Later, the press called him "Sleeping Sam" because he repeatedly slept through long sessions that bored him. In his usual frank manner, he also admitted that he did not know how to manage his own money, which made people question how he could oversee government budgets. He also fought to declare English the official

S. I. Hayakawa loved jazz music and wrote several papers and essays on the subject. He was born in Canada, but he attended graduate school in the United States.

language of the United States. Many people felt this move attacked America's diversity.

He made his most controversial statement when discussing the US government's decision to force Japanese Americans into internment camps during World War II. Historians today agree that wartime fear and racism drove the decision, and Japanese Americans did not pose a threat to the country. Not one had betrayed their country during wartime, and many Japanese Americans risked their lives fighting on behalf of the US during the war. Decades later, Japanese Americans began to demand reparations, or payment, for the losses they suffered while living in internment camps. Many had lost their homes, businesses, and personal belongings.

According to the *Washington Post*, Hayakawa, who was of Japanese ancestry, "angered many others when he defended the internment of 120,000 Japanese Americans during World War II as 'perhaps the best thing that could have happened.'" He said internment helped Japanese Americans better mix with the rest of society later. But Hayakawa, the *Post* noted,

Born in Budapest, Hungary, to a Jewish family, Tom Lantos was a Holocaust survivor. At the age of sixteen, he was arrested by the Nazis and sent to a labor camp.

"was a Canadian citizen teaching in Chicago during the war, and was not involved with the internment program."[5] So, how could he truly know about the struggles Japanese Americans in the camps faced?

In 1982, he decided not to run for reelection. He died in California in 1992 at the age of eighty-five.

TOM LANTOS

Tom Lantos was born February 1, 1928, to a Jewish family in Budapest, Hungary. In 1944, during World War II, the Nazi military occupied Hungary. They rounded up Tom and his family members and sent them to a labor camp. He was just sixteen years old.

Life in the labor camp was hard. The inmates were forced to work on projects that helped the Nazi cause. Tom escaped from the camp but was captured and badly beaten. He had better luck the second time he escaped. He managed to find a safe place to live in Budapest with his aunt. He tried to find the rest of his family, especially his mother, but could not. At that time, he joined the resistance movement, the group of people who worked against the Nazis. According to Biography.com, "Because of his 'Aryan' coloring (blond hair and blue eyes), he was able to move around Budapest in a military cadet's uniform, secretly delivering life-saving food and medicine to other Jews in various safe houses."[6]

Budapest was liberated in early 1945. Although Tom was free, he realized the terrible truth that his mother and other family members had died in the Holocaust. He tried to rebuild his life, as many Hungarians attempted to rebuild their war-torn nation. The Hillel foundation gave him a scholarship to travel to the United States, where he studied at the University of Washington and at the University of California. He earned a PhD in economics and taught at San Francisco State University.

In 1980, he entered politics by winning the election to serve in the US House of Representatives. A popular politician in his district (the Eleventh District, later changed to the Twelfth District), he won reelection thirteen times. He served on many important congressional committees, including serving as the chairman of the House Committee on Foreign Affairs.

When he retired in 2008, his colleagues in Congress praised him. He said, "It is only in the United States that a penniless survivor of the Holocaust and a fighter in the anti-Nazi underground could have received an education, raised a family and had the privilege of serving the last three decades of his life as a member of Congress." He added, "I will never be able to express fully my profoundly felt gratitude to this great country."[7]

TED LIEU

Ted Lieu was born in Taipei, Taiwan, on March 29, 1969. As a child, he moved to the United States, where he attended schools in Cleveland, Ohio. He later attended Stanford University and Georgetown University's law school. Lieu also served in the United States Air Force as a military prosecutor and earned the rank of colonel. Discussing his military service, Lieu said, "I joined the Air Force on active duty and decided to continue to serve in the Reserves to give back to America—an exceptional country of boundless opportunity that has given so much to my family."[8]

Californians elected Ted Lieu, a Taiwanese American, to the House of Representatives in 2014. He has been a fierce critic of President Trump.

Lieu started his career in politics by serving in the California State Legislature; later, he also won a seat in the California State Senate. In 2014, after Congressman Henry Waxman retired, he ran for his seat in the US House of Representatives. Lieu won the election and currently sits on two important congressional committees: the House Budget Committee and the House Oversight Committee.

THE KING OF "FIRSTS"

Dalip Singh Saund was the first Asian elected to the US Congress. He was born in in British India's Punjab Province in 1899. A member of the Sikh religion, Saund graduated with a degree in mathematics from University of the Punjab in Amritsar. He convinced his family to pay for a trip to the United States, where he planned to study and learn about the food canning industry. He wanted to return to India to open a food canning company there. In his autobiography, he wrote, "I assured my family that I would study in the United States for at least two and not more than three years and would then return home." [9]

He earned his doctorate degree in 1924 from the University of California at Berkeley, where he also became politically aware of the issues facing Indian immigrants in the United States. Saund became very attached to life in the United States and delayed his return to India. He became an American citizen in 1949.

In 1955, having had success in local elections and local politics, he ran for a seat in the US House of Representatives. He won and was reelected twice, serving in total from January 3, 1957, to January 3, 1963. His success earned Saund many "firsts." He was

(continued on page 40)

Dalip Saund poses next to a bust of President Abraham Lincoln. Saund, who was born in India, served in the US House of Representatives.

(continued from page 38)

the first Sikh American, the first Indian American, the first person born in Asia, and the first person of a non-Abrahamic faith (that is, he was not Christian, Jewish, or Muslim) to serve in the United States Congress.

Unfortunately, Saund's career was cut short in 1962, when he suffered a severe stroke. Though he survived, he was left disabled and unable to speak. He died in California in 1973.

Since the election of President Donald Trump, Lieu, a Democrat, has been very critical of the new administration. President Trump signed an executive order that banned the entry of people from seven nations that have large Muslim populations. Many of the people attempting to enter the United States were refugees fleeing from war and terrorism. Several courts overturned the ban. Trump tried revising it, but an appeals court still blocked it. Although the president has argued that the ban is necessary to keep Americans safe from terrorists, many critics have stated that it is based on bigotry and religious discrimination. As a result, supporters of the president have applauded the ban, while others consider it to be hateful.

Congressman Lieu said of the ban, "Trump is quick to tweet about who is American and who is un-American. As an immigrant, veteran, and member of Congress, I can tell you there is nothing more un-American than undermining our fundamental value of accepting those who are fleeing tyranny, those who want to start a better life in the United States."[10]

CHAPTER 3

IMMIGRANTS ON THE BENCH

Some of the most powerful Americans actually serve in the judiciary branch of government. People often don't think of judges as playing a political role, but judges and courts do shape politics simply by shaping the law. In fact, many political debates and problems often end up in court. The judges covered in this chapter belong to the large group of Americans who moved to the United States from foreign countries.

JAMES IREDELL

James Iredell was born in England in 1751, when the British Empire still ruled the United States colonies. His family was poor, so James accepted a government position in the American colonies to help his family financially. He was just seventeen years old when he made the voyage across the Atlantic Ocean to work as a customs comptroller in North Carolina. Also known as controller, a comptroller looks over the financial dealings of an organization, very much like an accountant.

Once James arrived in the colonies, he worked hard and also studied law. At first, he hoped to make enough money to become a lawyer and rejoin his family in England. But he ended up loving life in the Americas.

Born in England, James Iredell staunchly defended the new American government. George Washington appointed him to the first Supreme Court in 1790.

He became a lawyer in 1771 and took an interest in some of the colonists' complaints against King George III. Even though he still worked for the British crown, Iredell admitted that the colonists had reason to be concerned. In 1774, he wrote an essay called "To the Inhabitants of Great Britain" in which he tried to explain some of the colonists' complaints against the Crown. He followed this with another essay in 1775, "Principles of an American Whig." In this piece, he lists the colonists' charges against the Crown in a way that likely shaped the writing of the Declaration of Independence. In "Principles of an American Whig," he states:

"That government being only means of securing freedom and happiness to the people, whenever it deviates from this end, and their freedom and happiness are in great danger of being irrevocably lost, the government is no longer entitled to their allegiance, the only consideration for which it could be justly claimed or honorably pledged being basely and tyrannically withheld."[1]

He argues here that a government should serve the needs of its people. If it doesn't, then the people have the right to overthrow the rule of that government.

After the United States won independence from England, Iredell continued to serve North Carolina and his new country loyally. On February 8, 1790, President George Washington appointed him to the Supreme Court. He was only thirty-eight years old, the youngest of the first group of Supreme Court justices. He died ten years later, at the age of forty-eight, after suddenly falling ill.

GEORGE SUTHERLAND

Alexander George Sutherland was born on March 25, 1862, in Buckinghamshire, England. His parents moved to the United States when George was just a baby. He grew up with the Mormon community in Utah and attended Brigham Young Academy, graduating in 1881.

Alexander George Sutherland was born in England to a Scottish father and an English mother. He served in the US House of Representatives and the Senate, and later, on the Supreme Court.

He attended law school in Michigan for a year but returned to Utah to work for his father's law firm there. When Utah joined the union as a state in 1896, he served as a state senator, then later as a representative from Utah in the US House of Representatives. In 1905, he became a United States senator representing Utah.

After losing the 1916 Senate election, Sunderland remained in politics, serving as the president of the American Bar Association. While in Washington, DC, he became an advisor to President Warren G. Harding. The president appointed Sutherland to the Supreme Court in 1922.

As a justice, Sutherland opposed President Franklin D. Roosevelt's "New Deal" laws. He believed that it wasn't the government's job to create a welfare program and other safety nets for poor Americans. Sutherland and three other justices, nicknamed "the Four Horsemen" by their critics, succeeded in blocking Roosevelt's efforts until one of the four changed his vote.

Sutherland retired from the Supreme Court in 1938. According to John Fox, "Sutherland holds the distinction of having more opinions overruled than any other justice in the history of the Court."[2] But Sutherland was also known for being well spoken.

FELIX FRANKFURTER

Felix Frankfurter was born on November 15, 1882, to a Jewish family in Vienna, Austria. He moved to the United States as a teenager and settled with his family in New York. Although his family were poor, Frankfurter learned English quickly and did well in school.

He attended the City College of New York, graduating in 1902. He then attended Harvard University, where he graduated with a law degree in 1906. While working as a lawyer, he befriended Supreme Court Justice Oliver Wendell Holmes, Jr. He worked in a series of jobs, including serving as a professor at Harvard and assisting the secretary of war in Washington, DC, during World War I.

HOW THE COURT SYSTEM WORKS

The United States has a federal judicial system. The Supreme Court is the nation's highest court. Cases that the lower courts can't solve may end up before the Supreme Court justices.

Under the Supreme Court, there are thirteen appellate courts, known as the US Courts of Appeals. There are also ninety-four district courts, known as US District Courts. There is at least one district court in each of the fifty states, as well as in the District of Columbia, Puerto Rico, the US Virgin Islands, Guam, and the Northern Mariana Islands.

They are arranged into twelve circuits, each of which has an appellate court. One of the largest circuits, for example, is the Ninth Circuit, which covers the western portion of the United States and includes California, Arizona, Nevada, Idaho, Montana, Washington, Oregon, Alaska, and Hawaii.

According to the government's website on federal courts, "The appellate court's task is to determine whether or not the law was applied correctly in the trial court. Appeals courts consist of three judges and do not use a jury."[3]

After the war, he helped start the American Civil Liberties Union (ACLU). Today, the group continues to fight for the civil rights of Americans and remains a powerful voice in American life. But in the early 1900s, many people viewed Frankfurter's work with the ACLU as suspicious. Some government officials thought it meant that he had communist ties, a charge Frankfurter denied. He likely faced the charge because he was Jewish, and many American Jews belonged to the American Communist Party. But many Americans also were anti-Semitic, or prejudiced against Jews.

Born in Austria, Felix Frankfurter immigrated to the United States at the age of twelve. He helped establish the American Civil Liberties Union.

In 1939, President Franklin D. Roosevelt nominated Frankfurter to serve on the US Supreme Court. As a justice, he supported cases that were unpopular. For example, he voted that the internment of Japanese Americans during World War II was constitutional. He also voted for the controversial 1940 case *Minersville School District v. Gobitis.* In this case, the Supreme Court defended a school board decision that all students had to salute the American flag and recite the Pledge of Allegiance, despite their religious views or opinions. But Frankfurter also voted to racially desegregate schools in the nation's historic 1954 *Brown v. Board of Education* case. Desegregation meant allowing students of all racial backgrounds to attend school together.

In 1962, Frankfurter stepped down from the bench. The next year, he received the Presidential Medal of Freedom from President Lyndon Johnson. Frankfurter died in 1965. His legacy was complicated, but according to John Fox, Frankfurter "felt that a person's position in the world should be earned, and that once a person had succeeded, he should become a mentor, helping others rise according to their abilities."[4]

ADALBERTO JORDAN

Adalberto Jordan was born in Havana, Cuba, in 1961. He moved to the United States with his family in 1968. His family lived in Miami, Florida, in a large Cuban American community. Jordan attended the University of Miami, where he completed his law degree in 1987. He served as a law clerk from 1988 to 1989 for Sandra Day O'Connor, the first female justice on the Supreme Court.

After practicing in a private law firm for several years, he became an assistant United States attorney representing Florida. He began teaching law as an adjunct professor at his alma mater, the University of Miami.

Born in Havana, Cuba, Adalberto Jordan grew up in Miami, Florida. President Barack Obama appointed him to serve on the United States Court of Appeals for the Eleventh Circuit.

HOW CAN ONE BECOME A JUSTICE?

Most Americans know that the president of the United States must be a citizen by birth. Article II of the Constitution spells this out clearly: "No Person except a natural born Citizen, or a Citizen of the United States, at the time of the Adoption of this Constitution, shall be eligible to the Office of President." The Constitution also states that the president must be at least thirty-five years old and have lived in the United States for at least fourteen years.

However, this rule does not apply to justices who serve on the Supreme Court, which surprises many Americans. According to the Supreme Court's official website, "The Constitution does not specify qualifications for justices such as age, education, profession, or native-born citizenship. A justice does not have to be a lawyer or a law school graduate, but all justices have been trained in the law."

So, to serve on the Supreme Court, there are no real requirements except knowledge of the law. The president of the United States nominates justices to the Court, and the US Senate must approve the nomination. In this way, the Constitution allows for a selection process involving both the executive and legislative

The US Supreme Court is the highest court in the nation. It is part of the judicial branch of the American government, charged with interpreting the law.

branches. Appointments have no term limit. They are lifelong appointments, and justices either retire from the bench or die while serving in the position. [5]

In 1999, President Bill Clinton named him US District Court judge for the Southern District of Florida. President Barack Obama appointed him to the Eleventh Circuit, United States Court of Appeals, in 2012. On February 15 of that year, the United States Senate confirmed Jordan in a vote of 94–5. He continues to serve in that position currently.

RAYMOND LOHIER JR.

Raymond Lohier Jr. was born on December 1, 1965, in Montreal, Canada. His parents were Haitian immigrants. When he was young, his family moved to Philadelphia, Pennsylvania, where his mother opened a women's clothing store and his father was a doctor. Lohier attended the Friends Central School of Philadelphia and then Harvard University. He earned his law degree from New York University, where he served as editor-in-chief of the school's law journal, the *Annual Survey of American Law*. He also received a Vanderbilt Medal from NYU.

After law school, Lohier was a clerk for Judge Robert P. Patterson Jr. in the United States District Court for New York. He joined a law firm for a short time, then returned to public service when he was named assistant United States attorney in 2000. In 2009, he was chosen to serve as head of the Securities and Commodities Fraud Task Force. While in this position, Judge Lohier oversaw the investigation and prosecution of Bernard Madoff. The Madoff scandal rocked the financial world in late 2008, when Madoff admitted to committing fraud. Madoff was the former NASDAQ chairman and founder of Bernard L. Madoff Investment Securities, a well-known Wall Street firm. Lohier sentenced Madoff to 150 years in jail for running the largest Ponzi scheme in American history. It caused many people to lose their savings and investments.

Raymond Lohier, left, worked to help prosecute several high-profile insider trading and fraud cases. A Haitian American, he serves on the United States Court of Appeals for the Second Circuit.

In 2010, New York Senator Chuck Schumer nominated Lohier to be judge of the United States Court of Appeals for the Second Circuit. In his recommendation, Schumer said, "Mr. Lohier is not only a highly qualified candidate for the Second Circuit and a lawyer whose views have been tempered by a broad range of experiences, but, as a proud Haitian American, he is a candidate who would enhance the diversity of the federal bench."[6]

President Barack Obama nominated Lohier, who was approved with no dissenting votes, which means that the vote in favor of his nomination was unanimous. During his short time on the Second Circuit bench, Judge Lohier has worked on some famous cases.

According to Thomas Hopson, "In *New York State Rifle and Pistol Association v. Cuomo*, [Lohier] voted to uphold gun-control legislation in New York and Connecticut. The legislation, passed in the wake of the Sandy Hook shootings, prohibited possession of semiautomatic assault weapons and large-capacity magazines."[7]

He has also overseen other cases, such as the *United States v. Apple*, in which Apple worked to raise the price of e-books to compete with Amazon.com. The Second Circuit decided that Apple had committed a conspiracy and ruled against the company. Lohier wrote, "More corporate bullying is not an appropriate antidote to corporate bullying."[8]

CHAPTER 4

IMMIGRANTS IN THE GOVERNOR'S MANSION

State governors hold a large amount of power. The governor is the head of a state's executive branch, just as the president heads the nation's executive branch. In the United States, a person must be born in the country to serve as president, but no such law exists for governors. According to the National Governor's Association, "The requirement of US citizenship for gubernatorial candidates ranges from no formal provision to 20 years."[1]

JOHN DOWNEY

California's first non-American governor was John Downey. Born in Ireland in 1827, he arrived in the United States as an immigrant at the age of fifteen. He lived in Maryland for a time and then in Ohio. As a young man, he was unable to complete his education because his family didn't have much money. He began working as soon as he could.

He worked as a pharmacist, and in 1846, he and a business partner opened a pharmacy in Cincinnati. Downey heard about the gold rush in California. News of gold led many people to travel west, and Downey joined them. In 1849, he headed for California

This drawing depicts Chinese immigrant workers during California's gold rush in 1849. Hundreds of people moved to California, hoping to become rich.

but only mined for a short period of time.

Downey settled down in Los Angeles, where he opened a pharmacy with James P. McFarland. According to the California State Library, "His businesses did very well in Southern California, where the town of Downey is named after him."[2]

Downey became lieutenant governor of California in 1860 but became governor after just a few days when Milton Latham resigned from the role. Latham, who had only served as governor for five days, wanted to be a senator instead. As governor, Downey became quite popular for making strong decisions. For example, "[his] veto of the 'bulkhead' bill, which would have allowed ownership of San Francisco's waterfront by a monopoly, made Downey a hero."[3]

OCTAVIANO AMBROSIO LARRAZOLO

Octaviano Ambrosio Larrazolo was a governor of New Mexico and the first Hispanic American to serve in the United States Senate.

He was born on December 7, 1859, in Allende in the Mexican state of Chihuahua. At this time, the French controlled Mexico. Many Mexicans wanted to be free of French rule, and Octaviano's parents, wealthy landowners, felt the same. French soldiers harassed them because of their support of an independent Mexico.

When he was eleven years old, Octaviano moved to the United States to study as a student of a French bishop, J.B. Salpoint. The bishop sent the young boy to Arizona. As Roman Catholics, his parents felt that this would be a good opportunity for their son. They had provided him with a good education in their home.

From Arizona, Octaviano eventually moved to New Mexico, where he attended St. Michael's College in Santa Fe and completed his studies there in 1877. He had originally planned to become a priest because he'd studied theology and the church, but he decided to become a teacher instead. For a short time, Larrazolo worked in Tucson, Arizona, but then moved to Texas, where he taught and served as a school principal for several years.

The Rio Grande flows near Taos, New Mexico. It is one of the principal rivers in the southwestern United States and forms a natural border with Mexico.

During this time, he became interested in American politics and law. He began studying the law, reading and working late into the night after long days teaching. He decided to become a lawyer, but he had to become a US citizen to do so. He became a citizen in 1884 at age twenty-five. After serving several court clerkships, he became a lawyer in Texas in 1888. For several years, he served as a district attorney for the state of Texas.

He moved back to the territory of New Mexico, where he had studied and worked for so long, in 1895. At the time, New Mexico was the name for all lands in the United States north of the Rio Grande River. The United States had seized the territory in 1848 as a result of the Mexican-American War. The United States purchased the land from Mexico in what is known as the Gadsen Purchase of 1853.

New Mexico wouldn't become a US state until 1912. Before that time, Larrazolo was living and working in the territory, and he stood up for the large population of people who were of Mexican ancestry and spoke Spanish. He worried that when New Mexico entered the Union as the forty-seventh state, the government wouldn't respect the rights of this population.

He had every right to think this might happen. At the time, the government denied rights to another group of people—African Americans. After the Civil War ended in 1865, enslaved African Americans became free, but the government stripped them of their civil rights. A group of state and federal laws, known as Jim Crow laws, allowed white Americans to discriminate against fellow black citizens. Larrazolo feared that Mexican Americans would also suffer from discrimination if the laws of the new state of New Mexico didn't protect them.

Larrazolo used his legal expertise to help make sure certain measures appeared in the constitution of New Mexico. Elected as a delegate to the constitutional convention in 1911, he made sure to fight for these measures, which included a ban on segregating schools (a policy in many parts of the US that allowed states to provide a lower standard of education to African American students). He also insisted that teachers could speak both Spanish and English in public schools.

According to Suzanne Stamatov, "When writing the articles on the Bill of Rights, Education and the Elective Franchise, Larrazolo and others deemed it essential to guarantee the political, civil, and religious rights of those of Spanish and Mexican descent. The resulting constitution made it unique among the American states."[4]

Larrazolo had been a Democrat, but the way Democrats tried to block these measures at the convention upset him. As a result, he decided to leave the Democratic Party and become a Republican.

As a Republican, he was electedf governor of New Mexico in 1918. Stamatov points out that he was a leader with morals. He often voted on things based on whether or not he felt they were right and just, not whether they would be popular decisions. For example, she notes, Larrazolo "vigorously supported the ratification of the nineteenth amendment even though his core constituency of Spanish-speaking New Mexicans opposed women's suffrage."[5] He also worked hard for racial justice in his state at a time when standing up for racial minority groups proved unpopular.

He didn't serve as governor again. Instead, he ran for a seat in the United States Senate. He won in 1928 but only served until his death in 1930.

NEVADA'S GOVERNORS

Nevada entered the Union in 1864, becoming the thirty-sixth state. Several of its early leaders were immigrants. To date, Nevada has had three foreign-born governors, all of whom served in the last decade of the 1800s.

(continued on page 63)

Nevada became the thirty-sixth state in 1864. This photo depicts Swift's Station, located at Carson and Lake Bigler Road, on the eastern summit of the Sierra Nevada.

(continued from page 61)

Frank Bell was born in Toronto, Canada, in 1840. He arrived in the United States to work on the construction of the transcontinental telegraph. (A telegraph is a long-distance communications system that works by transmitting information by wire.) Bell served as acting governor from 1890 to 1891 and was the first foreign-born head of state.

John Edward Jones was born in 1840 in Montgomeryshire, Wales. He arrived in the United States with his family as a teenager, settling first in Iowa before arriving in Nevada to work on the Union Pacific Railroad in 1869. He was elected governor in 1895 but died in office on April 10, 1896.

Reinhold Sadler served as acting governor after Jones' death. He was born in 1848 in Czarnikau, Prussia. Sadler served the rest of Jones' term, winning election in his own right in 1898. He served until 1902.

JOHN MOSES

John Moses was born on June 12, 1885, in Strand, Norway. At the time, Strand was a small town with a booming fishing and shipping industry because of its location on the North Atlantic Ocean. He attended school in the national capital of Oslo and moved to the United States in 1905. He settled in Minnesota, where he found work as a farm laborer before taking an interest in the law.

Moses eventually moved to North Dakota, which became the thirty-ninth state in the Union in 1889. As a new state, North Dakota was growing and offered an eager, young immigrant many opportunities. In fact, the number of foreign-born Americans who settled in North Dakota made up a large part of the population in the early 1900s. These immigrants flocked to the new state because they could get farmland to work for income.

Moses was part of this immigrant population. In 1915, he earned a degree from the University of North Dakota's law school. That same year, he began practicing law in the state. He served as the state's attorney of Mercer County from 1919 to 1923 and again from 1927 to 1933.

The political life attracted him, and he ran for governor in 1936 but lost the election. He ran again two years later and won. He took office on January 5, 1939, as the twenty-second governor of North Dakota.

Moses won reelection as governor two more times. According to the North Dakota State Historical Society, "Moses' administration was a time of prosperity for the state. Rainfall was plentiful and there was a ready market for agriculture products. Moses was a popular governor. During his election campaign he gave speeches in English, German, or Norwegian, depending on his audience."[6]

He ran for a Senate seat in 1944, but he only served for two months—from January 3, 1945, until his death on March 3, 1945.

John Moses, born in Norway, served as a governor of North Dakota. A popular politician, he spoke three languages: English, German, and Norwegian.

ARNOLD SCHWARZENEGGER

Arnold Schwarzenegger is well known both in politics and in Hollywood. The action star served as the thirty-eighth governor of California.

He was born July 30, 1947, in Thal, Austria. As a youth, he became passionate about competitive bodybuilding. By his teens, he'd won many awards. And at the age of twenty, he made headlines by becoming the youngest person to be named Mr. Universe. His rise in the bodybuilding world made him famous, but it also led to positive publicity for the sport.

Schwarzenegger moved to the United States in 1968, where he continued his bodybuilding career. He won several more Mr. Universe titles as well as Mr. Olympia titles. Soon, he turned his attention to Hollywood, hoping to become an actor.

At first, he used the name Arnold Strong but later decided to use his birth name, which many Americans likely found hard to pronounce. He used his bodybuilding fame to help him win acting roles. In 1977, he starred in the film *Stay Hungry* with actress Sally Field. That year, he won a Golden Globe award for New Male Star of the Year.

He had his first major hit movie when he starred in 1982's *Conan the Barbarian*. In 1984, he starred in *Terminator*, one of his most famous film roles. He has a long list of hit movies, including sequels to *Terminator* and the films *Total Recall, True Lies, Predator,* and *The Expendables*. He also worked to promote physical activity. In 1990, President George H. W. Bush named him the chairman of the President's Council on Physical Fitness and Sports. At the time, President Bush said, "I have asked Arnold to chair the Council because I believe he is uniquely qualified to address and influence national health and fitness issues, especially among our youth."[7]

Born in Austria, Arnold Schwarzenegger began his career as a professional bodybuilder. He entered politics in the early 2000s, becoming the governor of California in 2003.

In 2003, California held a special recall election to replace Governor Gray Davis. In recall elections, voters don't have to wait for the next election cycle to vote out a politician who has lost their support. In this case, voters elected Arnold Schwarzenegger to replace Governor Gray Davis. Schwarzenegger had competition in the race, but the other candidates lacked his name recognition.

In his first speech as governor, Schwarzenegger said, "When I became a citizen 20 years ago, I had to take citizenship test. I had to learn about the history and the principles of our republic. What I learned, and I've never forgotten, is sovereignty rests with the people, not the government."[8]

WISCONSIN

James O. Davidson was born February 10, 1854, in Sogn, Norway. His family moved to the United States when Davidson was eighteen years old. He started out working as a farmhand and a tailor but later became a businessman.

Eventually, he entered politics, winning a seat in Wisconsin's State Assembly. He then served as state treasurer. In 1902, he became Robert LaFollette's lieutenant governor. When LaFollette resigned in 1906 to become a senator, Davidson replaced him. He won the next election in his own right and served until 1910.

According to the National Governors Association, "During Davidson's tenure, state regulation of the railroads was extended to include public utilities, telegraph, telephone, electricity, water companies, and the insurance industry."[9]

Schwarzenegger won reelection in 2006. While he was governor, he donated his salary to various charities. He left politics when his second term ended in 2010. He continues to act and take part in a variety of social causes, such as the Special Olympics and Habitat for Humanity.

This print features a depiction of Mosel, Germany, which takes its name from the Mosel River. Mosel was the home of Julius Peter Heil, an American politician and businessman.

JULIUS PETER HEIL

Julius Peter Heil was born in Mosel, Germany, in 1876. He moved to the United States with his family when he was five years old. He grew up to become a successful businessman.

Heil started the Heil Rail Joint Company, which was later known as the Heil Company. His political career took off after he won Wisconsin's 1938 race for governor. Heil served until 1942, when he lost an election for a third term. Afterward, he returned to the business world and once again served as the head of the Heil Company.

CHAPTER 5

IMMIGRANTS IN CITY HALL

The mayors of American cities and towns have long been as diverse as their populations. The US has a rich history of foreign-born mayors who made a home in the United States.

WILLIAM RUSSELL GRACE

William Russell Grace was born on May 10, 1832, in Cobh, Ireland. Since his family was wealthy, William lived very well. But he wanted to be independent and decided to move to the United States. His father objected, but Grace left anyway, sailing on a ship across the Atlantic at the age of fourteen.

Landing in New York, he struggled to find work. He made a living working for a printer and a shoemaker. He returned to Ireland in 1848. Three years later, he sailed with his father to Peru to look into a business project and ended up staying in the country and worked as a shipping clerk for the John Bryce Company. A few years later, Grace rose through the company's ranks. The name even changed to Bryce, Grace & Company. Eventually, Grace became owner and renamed the business W. R. Grace and Company. The business oversaw much of the shipping along the coastline of Peru and Chile.

Grace left Peru in 1865 after turning over the company to his brother. By then, Grace was

William R. Grace was born in Ireland. In 1880, he was elected mayor of New York, becoming the city's first Irish Catholic mayor.

independently wealthy. After moving to New York, Grace started the W.R. Grace Company in that city as well. He then ran for mayor of New York City and won the election in 1880, becoming the city's first Irish American and Roman Catholic mayor. He improved many of the city's institutions and lowered taxes on residents.

He never forgot about the country of his birth. When the Great Famine hit Ireland, he spent a small fortune in 1880 to ship food to the Irish people.

When France shipped the Statue of Liberty to America, Mayor Grace received the gift.

Grace died in New York City in 1904.

THE IRISH POTATO FAMINE

Ireland's Great Famine began in 1845, when the potato crop failed several years in a row. Ruled by the British, the Irish were already mostly poor. They depended on the potato as their main crop. It was nutritious, cheap, and easy to grow. When their crops failed, entire families starved.

Even worse, Irish farmers, most of whom worked as tenants on British-owned land, faced eviction when they could not pay their rents. Entire families, who had lived in shabby, rundown homes, now found themselves homeless. About one million people died of starvation and disease.

The Irish began leaving the country in large numbers. From 1845 to 1855, almost two million Irish men, women, and children traveled to the United States. They arrived poor and desperate and faced discrimination for being Catholics. They fought for jobs and crowded together in cheap, shared housing. But in time, they adapted to life in the United States.

VINCENT IMPELLITTERI

Vincenzo Impellitteri was born on February 4, 1900, in Sicily, Italy. The following year, his family moved to the United States and settled in Connecticut, where Vincenzo grew up and attended school. His father was a shoe cobbler, and the family struggled financially. Impellitteri became a citizen in 1922.

During World War I, he joined the US Navy. He later attended law school at Fordham University and worked at night as a hotel bellboy to pay his tuition. After graduating, he moved to New York City, where he worked as an assistant district attorney. He frowned upon mob activity and corruption. In 1945, he became president of the city council, a role he served in for five years.

Then, in 1950, the New York mayor accepted a position as ambassador to Mexico. Based on city rules, Impellitteri automatically became acting mayor. Politicians from the group known as Tammany Hall later tried to ruin his bid for election, but Impellitteri, running as an independent candidate, won the race. He ran under the slogan "unbought and unbossed."

As the *New York Times* put it, "In an era of flamboyant politicians and corruption scandals, Mr. Impelliteri—deliberate, scholarly, mild to the point of shyness—struck a responsive chord with New York voters and became the first person to become mayor of New York without the support of a major political party."[1]

He did not win reelection due to a series of scandals the city faced at the time he took office, which complicated his term as mayor. He went into private practice as a lawyer and died in 1987.

Vincent Impellitteri was an Italian American politician. He was born to a poor family in Sicily. His father was a shoe cobbler, and the family always struggled financially.

CARLOS GIMÉNEZ

Carlos Giménez is the mayor of Miami-Dade County, Florida. It is the state's largest county and one of America's most diverse and populated areas. Indeed, Giménez oversees a government structure of 26,000 employees and a $7 billion yearly budget.

As mayor of Miami-Dade County, Florida, Giménez oversees the state's largest county. Miami-Dade is one of the most diverse and populated areas in the United States.

Giménez was born in Cuba on January 17, 1954. He moved with his family to Miami, Florida, in 1960 after the Cuban Revolution and the rise of Fidel Castro. Many Cubans fled their homeland to escape communist rule.

Giménez attended high school in Miami, then earned a degree in public administration from Barry University. He joined the Miami Fire Department as a firefighter in the 1970s. The department promoted him to Fire Chief in 1991. Giménez then attended Harvard University, where he completed the program for senior executives in state and local government at the John F. Kennedy School of Government.

In 2000, he became the city manager of Miami, a role that required him to provide services to the city's residents. A few years later, he became county commissioner. In June 2011, he was elected Miami-Dade mayor in a recall vote that saw Carlos Alvarez step down.

Giménez is a generally popular mayor but became involved in a controversy in 2017. After President Donald Trump said he would take away federal funding from sanctuary cities, Giménez agreed to no longer make his city a safe haven for immigrants. American cities that welcome refugees and undocumented immigrants are known as sanctuary cities. In such cities, police do not help immigration agents track down undocumented immigrants.

Some politicians believe that sanctuary cities promote the breaking of the law, while leaders of such cities claim that most immigrants pose no threat to society. Giménez's decision to follow federal law has earned him sharp criticism. Many Miami-Dade leaders representing immigrants and minority groups "blasted Gimenez's decision…to comply with President Donald Trump's threatened, nativist ban on 'sanctuary cities,' which protect undocumented immigrants from deportation."[2]

MAYOR-MAKER

It would be difficult to find a more colorful character in American politics than Richard Croker. He was born November 24, 1843, in County Cork, Ireland, and moved to the United States as a child. The family lived in New York City, and they struggled to make a living. Richard often found himself in trouble, as he cared little for school and spent much of his time on the streets. He became involved with a group known as the Fourth Avenue Tunnel Gang.

Croker joined Tammany Hall, the New York political organization that had a large hand in running the Democratic Party in New York. It was responsible for helping scores of Irish immigrants adjust to life and do well in the United States. It provided legal and other services that helped immigrants. As a result, immigrants promised their political support to Tammany Hall. But the group also became known for corruption.

Croker rose through the ranks of Tammany Hall and the New York political scene. He served as an alderman, New York City fire commissioner, and city chamberlain. He was also elected New York City coroner, but he shot and killed his opponent on Election Day. He avoided a conviction for the killing, but the incident led him to have a tough reputation. In 1886, he was named grand sachem, or leader, of Tammany Hall. He helped many politicians win election, including New York City mayor Robert A. Van Wyck in 1897.

Croker stepped down from the position in 1906. He died in Ireland in 1922.

Richard Croker was born in County Cork, Ireland, on November 24, 1843. He was a small child when his family immigrated to the United States.

TOMÁS PEDRO REGALADO

While Giménez is the mayor of Miami-Dade County, the city of Miami also has a mayor. Tomás Pedro Regalado serves in this role. He was born on May 24, 1947, in Cuba.

Regalado's father was a lawyer and a journalist who was a prisoner of the communist government for twenty-two years. Tomás was fourteen when he arrived in the United States. He and his younger brother were part of a program known as Operation Peter Pan. The Catholic Welfare Bureau ran the program with the goal to relocate young children from the island. The program saw thousands of young Cubans flown off the island between 1960 and 1962 and taken to the United States without their parents.

The young Regalado brothers lived with an aunt until their mother could leave Cuba and join them. Regalado did well in school and became interested in journalism, like his father. He worked as a reporter for several television and radio stations and even

Tomás Pedro Regalado, the Cuban-born mayor of Miami, Florida, speaks at the Annie Miami Walk of Fame Ceremony at Bayside Marketplace in 2014.

served as the Latin American news editor for NBC. He also wrote a weekly column for the *Miami Herald.*

His journalism career was wildly successful. He interviewed presidents and government officials, covered wars and crises in foreign countries, and addressed the United Nations Human Rights Commission about human rights abuses in Cuba.

His father was released from prison in Cuba in 1979 and moved to Miami to live with his family. The Regalados had finally been reunited.

In 1996, Regalado was elected city commissioner of Miami, where he helped manage a financial crisis the city faced. In 2008, he was elected mayor of the city of Miami with 72 percent of the vote. He continues to be popular and has openly criticized the decision of Carlos Giménez to comply with federal laws about undocumented immigrants.

CHAPTER 6

DIPLOMATS AND ACTIVISTS

Public opinion about Henry Kissinger, a German American diplomat and advisor, has long been divided. During a February 2016 Democratic primary debate, opponents Hillary Clinton and Bernie Sanders argued about Kissinger, who had been out of the political scene for decades. During the debate, Clinton pointed out that Kissinger supported her candidacy.

In return, Sanders said, "I happen to believe that Henry Kissinger was one of the most destructive secretaries of state in the modern history of this country." Clinton answered by saying that she listened to the opinions of many people, including Kissinger. He is a friend of both Hillary Clinton and former president Bill Clinton.

But Sanders, in a loud, mocking voice, replied, "I am proud to say that Henry Kissinger is not my friend!"[1]

Who is Henry Kissinger, and why was he still so hotly debated decades after his political service to the nation?

Heinz Alfred Kissinger was born on May 27, 1923, in Furth, Germany. His family was Jewish, and anti-Semitism began to spread throughout the country at this time. Nazi youth gangs often beat and bullied Heinz, and his family suffered several forms of

President Richard Nixon walks with one of his key advisors, Henry Kissinger, in 1972. Kissinger, a German native, remains a controversial figure in American politics.

discrimination. For example, young Heinz did well in school but a very good high school rejected him from attending because he was Jewish.

In 1938, when Heinz was fifteen, the Kissingers fled to the United States, barely escaping the Holocaust.

Although he had to work to help his family, who lived in poverty during their early years in the United States, Heinz excelled in school. He learned English quickly and attended college. He became a US citizen in 1943, but the country had entered the war by then. The government drafted him. According to Biography. com, "Thus, just five years after he left, Kissinger found himself back in his homeland of Germany, fighting the very Nazi regime from which he had once fled."[2] Later, he told a reporter that serving in the war made him feel American. In Germany, he had never felt at home because he was Jewish. "I look back at those years with great pride," Kissinger said.[3]

After the war, Kissinger decided to study political science and history. He enrolled in Harvard University in 1947 and graduated with highest honors in 1950. He stayed at Harvard for a PhD, which he earned in 1954. Harvard hired him as a professor in the Department of Government, where he remained until 1969. He wrote several important books about war and policy, which earned him a reputation as a highly intelligent person.

In 1961, John F. Kennedy became president, and many Americans felt more hopeful than they had in quite some time. Kennedy appointed Kissinger to serve as a special foreign policy advisor. Kissinger continued in the role when Lyndon B. Johnson became president after Kennedy's assassination. In 1969, Richard Nixon won the presidential election by promising to help America find a better way to move forward in the Vietnam War.

Kennedy, Johnson, and finally Richard Nixon all had to face Vietnam, while Americans at home protested America's involvement with more and more anger. According to Robert K. Brigham, "Protests erupted on college campuses and in major cities at first, but by 1968 every corner of the country seemed to have felt the war's impact. Perhaps one of the most famous incidents in the anti-war movement was the police riot in Chicago during the 1968 Democratic National Convention. Hundreds of thousands of people came to Chicago in August 1968 to protest American intervention in Vietnam and the leaders of the Democratic Party who continued to prosecute the war."[4]

Kissinger was a key figure in the Nixon administration. According to Biography.com, "As National Security Advisor from 1969–75, and then as Secretary of State from 1973–77, Kissinger would prove one of the most dominant, influential and controversial statesmen in American history."[5]

Nixon had promised to end America's involvement in the war. Kissinger advised him, however, to make many unpopular moves. For example, according to Brigham, "The Nixon years also saw the expansion of the war into neighboring Laos and Cambodia, violating the international rights of these countries in secret campaigns, as the White House tried desperately to rout out Communist sanctuaries and supply routes."[6] The bombing of Cambodia was so intense— hundreds of thousands of Cambodians died—that protests spread all over the world and especially in the United States.

Despite this, Nixon continued to rely on aerial bombings to stop the northern forces. Kissinger's critics, then and now, question why he thought that the US military had the right to conduct those illegal bombings. Viet Thanh Nguyen, a Vietnam War survivor and American Pulitzer Prize winner, wrote, "What Kissinger's perspective

On October 15, 1969, a massive demonstration was held on Boston Common. The crowd of approximately 100,000 demanded an end to the Vietnam War.

reveals is a belief that the rule of law is determined by the rule of power. The most powerful state—the one most capable of inflicting violence—dictates what is lawful."[7]

Later in the war, Kissinger tried to create a peace agreement, but it failed. The war finally ended when North Vietnamese forces spread out to South Vietnam and took the capital of Saigon on April 30, 1975.

VIETNAM

The Vietnam War is known as the Second Indochina War, and it was the result of a long, colonial battle between France and Vietnam. It began in 1954, when France ended its colonial rule over Vietnam. The Geneva Peace Accords, however, decided that Vietnam should be split into North and South Vietnam. In 1956, elections took place to unite the country. Fearing that the Communist Party in Vietnam would have too much power, the United States, under President Eisenhower, supported the South Vietnamese party that opposed the revolution.

By providing military and economic aid, the US helped to start a completely new nation, South Vietnam. Ngo Dinh Diem, who was strongly anti-communist, led the new country. Fights took place between the largely communist North Vietnamese and the pro-American South Vietnamese. The communists hoped to unify the country through political, peaceful means, but Diem proved to be harsh in his treatment of pro-communist South Vietnamese citizens.

In return, the North Vietnamese began to use violent tactics to battle South Vietnam. Meanwhile, the United States kept sinking more and more deeply into the war, unable to get out until Saigon finally fell in 1975.

After the war, Kissinger worked to ease the tensions of the Cold War between the United States and communist nations like the Soviet Union and China. After Nixon's impeachment and resignation from office, Kissinger continued to be a valued advisor to President Gerald Ford and President Ronald Reagan. He fought for unpopular actions that earned him criticism, such as the United States' involvement in the overthrow and murder of Chilean leader Salvador Allende in 1973. Kissinger supported the next Chilean leader, Augusto Pinochet. But Pinochet ended up committing human rights crimes against Chileans during his dictatorship from 1973 to 1990.

All in all, Kissinger has certainly earned himself a complicated reputation. His supporters feel that he made the necessary moves to preserve the interests of the United States around the world, but his critics believe he didn't value human rights for people around the world. This led him to make terrible decisions on behalf of the American government, critics say.

MADELEINE ALBRIGHT

Madeleine Albright was born Marie Jana Korbelová on May 15, 1937, in Prague, Czechoslovakia (now the Czech Republic). Her father, Joseph Korbel, was a diplomat for the Czech government. She moved with her family to England when she was a child because of Nazi violence during World War II. Her parents were Jews but converted to Catholicism in order to escape persecution. However, several other family members, including three of her grandparents, died in the Holocaust.

After the war, Madeleine's parents moved back to Prague, and her father became the ambassador to Yugoslavia, which was giving way to communism. She attended schools in Switzerland to avoid this change. There, she learned French and changed her name from Marie Jana to Madeleine. When Communists took over Yugoslavia,

Born in the Czech Republic, Madeleine Albright immigrated to the United States in 1948. President Bill Clinton appointed her to become the first female US Secretary of State.

her father sent the family to the United States.

The family moved in 1948, living first in New York and then in Denver. Her father became a professor at the University of Denver, where one of his students was Condoleezza Rice (who later served in President George W. Bush's administration). In the United States, Madeleine attended American schools and later graduated from Wellesley College and Columbia University, where she earned a PhD in public law and government. She married Joseph Albright after graduating from Wellesley. His family was powerful in the publishing world.

Albright was very talented and wise beyond her years, which helped her win key political positions. She served on the National Security Council during the administration of President Jimmy Carter. Albright became an advisor to presidential candidate Michael Dukakis in 1988. Five years later, she represented the United States in the United Nations, appointed by President Bill Clinton.

Albright became known as a leader. In 1996, President Clinton appointed her secretary of state, and the Senate approved her nomination unanimously. She was the first woman ever to hold that position, opening the door for other women who followed—Condoleezza Rice and Hillary Clinton. According to Biography.com, "In her new role, Albright quickly lived up to her reputation as a strong-willed and outspoken problem-solver, engaging with a broad range of issues."[8]

She left the position in 2001 and became involved in various business and political projects, such as launching a global strategy company, the Albright Stonebridge Group. She also authored several books, including a memoir of her years as secretary of state and a memoir about her Prague childhood. In 2012, President Barack Obama gave her the Presidential Medal of Freedom.

In 2016, she campaigned for Hillary Clinton, who ran for president. Clinton was the first woman to win a major party nomination, but she lost the election to Donald Trump.

ELAINE CHAO

Elaine Chao was born on March 26, 1953, in Taiwan. She moved to the United States with her family at age eight. In 1975, she graduated from Mount Holyoke College. Later, in 1979, she earned a business degree from Harvard University.

President George H. W. Bush named her deputy secretary of transportation in 1989. For several years, she worked in a number of roles, including leading the Peace Corps and chairing the United Way of America. The United Way is a nonprofit organization that seeks to improve education, income, and health services to all Americans through community and fundraising work.

In 2001, President George W. Bush, the son of George H. W. Bush, appointed her US secretary of labor. She was the first Asian American woman to serve in a presidential cabinet, and she stayed in that position until the end of President Bush's second term in 2009.

Currently, she is serving as the transportation secretary in the administration of President Donald Trump. The Senate challenged many of Trump's appointees during the approval process but not Chao. CNN reported, "The Senate voted overwhelmingly Tuesday to approve Elaine Chao as secretary of transportation. The vote was 93 to 6."[9]

In 2017, Elaine Chao became the eighteenth US transportation secretary. In addition to being the first Asian American woman appointed to a president's cabinet, she is also the first Taiwanese American.

PRAMILA JAYAPAL

Pramila Jayapal was born in Chennai, India, on September 21, 1965, but she grew up in Indonesia and Singapore. At the age of sixteen, she moved to the United States to study at Georgetown University. After graduation, she studied at Northwestern University, where she earned an MBA degree. She became an American citizen in 2000. One year later, terrorists attacked her new country.

After the September 11, 2001, attacks on the United States, Jayapal found rising prejudice against immigrants disturbing. She became interested in civil rights work, focused on improving the political climate for immigrants. She founded Hate Free Zone, which later changed its name to OneAmerica, With Justice for All. The mission of the organization states: "OneAmerica advances the fundamental principles of democracy and justice at the local, state and national levels by building power within immigrant communities in collaboration with key allies."[10]

Born in India in 1965, Pramila Jayapal lives in the state of Washington. She serves as the US representative for Washington's Seventh Congressional District.

Jayapal started the organization because she felt that the public viewed Muslim, Arab, and Indian immigrants with suspicion. "When Sept. 11 happened, I just thought to myself that everything is going to change for people who look like me," Jayapal said. She added, "For the next few days, I didn't want to wear my normal clothes, I didn't want my son to go out…it was so awful…I just thought there must be something we could do about this intolerance."[11]

As an immigration attorney, Jayapal used her experience to help others. As part of her organization, she turned to other attorneys willing to work for free to help immigrants fight for their rights and avoid deportation. The organization was successful and continues its work today.

Jayapal has won praise as a leader. In 2002, she earned the Distinguished Citizen Award for Human Rights presented by the Seattle mayor's office. *Seattle Magazine* named her one of its "25 Most Influential People" in 2004. Three years later, the *Puget Sound Business Journal* named her a "Woman of Influence."

Jayapal also wrote two books about her experiences as an immigrant: *Pilgrimage to India: A Woman Revisits Her Homeland* and *A Woman Alone: Travel Tales from Around the Globe*. She gave a popular TED Talk about how immigration can challenge people's fear and xenophobia, which is a fear of foreigners.

Jayapal has played an active role in Washington state politics. She helped to negotiate a $15 minimum wage for the city of Seattle's workers. In 2014, she was elected to the Washington State Senate. Two years later, she ran for a seat in the US House of Representatives. Bernie Sanders, US senator and 2016 presidential candidate, endorsed her. Jayapal won the congressional election and currently represents the Seventh District of Washington.

She has been an outspoken critic of President Trump, who issued a ban on travel from several Muslim-majority countries in 2017. Jayapal said of the ban, "President Trump is once again attempting to shut America's door to immigrants and vulnerable refugees who are fleeing war-ravaged countries. This 'do-over' order still has consequences that stretch far and wide and hurt our national security."[12]

CHAPTER NOTES

CHAPTER 1

1. "William Paterson," Biography.com, http://www.biography.com/people/william-paterson-9434637#synopsis.
2. "William Paterson," Bioguide.com, http://bioguide.congress.gov/scripts/biodisplay.pl?index=p000102.
3. "US Immigration Before 1965," History.com, http://www.history.com/topics/u-s-immigration-before-1965.
4 "William Paterson," Bioguide.com.
5. "US Immigration Before 1965."
6. "Albert Gallatin," Britannica.com, https://www.britannica.com/biography/Albert-Gallatin.
7. Ibid.
8. Ibid.
9. "Pierre Soule," Bioguide.com, http://bioguide.congress.gov/scripts/biodisplay.pl?index=s000682.
10. "William Paterson," Bioguide.com, http://bioguide.congress.gov/scripts/biodisplay.pl?index=p000102
11. J. Preston Moore, "Pierre Soulé: Southern Expansionist and Promoter," *Journal of Southern History*, http://www.latinamericanstudies.org/filibusters/Pierre-Soule.pdf.
12. "Knute Nelson," MNopedia.org, http://www.mnopedia.org/person/nelson-knute-1843-1923.

CHAPTER 2

1. Theodore Saloutos, "The Rise of the Equity Cooperative Exchange," *The Mississippi Valley Historical Review*, June 1945.
2. "Magnus Johnson," Bioguide.com, http://bioguide.congress.gov/scripts/biodisplay.pl?index=J000161.
3. JY Smith, "Outspoken US Senator SI Hayakawa Dies at 85," *Washington Post*. February 28, 1992, https://www.washingtonpost.com/

archive/local/1992/02/28/outspoken-us-senator-si-hayakawa-dies-at-85/761fdf45-6557-4b88-99fc-1a66d5628e43/?utm_term=.d3ee9b067348.

4. "Ex-Sen. Hayakawa Dies; Unpredictable Iconoclast," *Los Angeles Times*, February 28, 1992, http://articles.latimes.com/1992-02-28/news/mn-2960_1_state-college.

5. Smith, "Outspoken US Senator."

6. "Tom Lantos," Biography.com, http://www.biography.com/people/tom-lantos-270367#growing-up-during-the-holocaust.

7. Ibid.

8. "Congressman Lieu Statement on Promotion to Colonel, US Air Force Reserves," House.gov, December 9, 2015, https://lieu.house.gov/media-center/press-releases/congressman-lieu-statement-promotion-colonel-us-air-force-reserves.

9. Tom Patterson, "Triumph and Tragedy of Dalip Saund," *California Historian*, June 1992, http://www.pbs.org/rootsinthesand/i_dalip1.html.

10. "Rep. Lieu Statement on Second Muslim Travel Ban," House.gov, March 6, 2017, https://lieu.house.gov/media-center/press-releases/rep-lieu-statement-trumps-second-muslim-travel-ban.

CHAPTER 3

1. "Principles of an American Whig," North Carolina History Project, http://northcarolinahistory.org/encyclopedia/principles-of-an-american-whig/.

2. John Fox, "George Sutherland," PBS.org, http://www.pbs.org/wnet/supremecourt/capitalism/robes_sutherland.html.

3. "Court Role and Structure," USCourts.gov, http://www.uscourts.gov/about-federal-courts/court-role-and-structure.

4. John Fox, "Felix Frankfurter," PBS.org, http://www.pbs.org/wnet/supremecourt/rights/robes_frankfurter.html.

5. "Frequently Asked Questions," Supreme Court.gov, https://www. supremecourt.gov/faq.aspx#faqgi2.
6. Ashby Jones, "From U.S. Attorney's Office to Second Circuit for Ray Lohier?" *Wall Street Journal,* February 10, 2010, http://blogs. wsj.com/law/2010/02/10/from-us-attorneys-office-to-second-circuit-for-raymond-lohier/.
7. Thomas Hopson, "Raymond Lohier, Former Federal Prosecutor," Scotusblog.com, March 8, 2016, http://www.scotusblog. com/2016/03/potential-nominee-raymond-lohier-former-federal-prosecutor/.
8. Ibid.

CHAPTER 4

1. "Qualifications and Tenure," National Governor's Association, https://www.nga.org/cms/home/management-resources/ governors-powers-and-authority.html#qualifications.
2. "John Downey 1860-1862," California State Library, http:// governors.library.ca.gov/07-downey.html.
3. Ibid.
4. Suzanne Stamatov, "Octaviano Ambrosio Larrazolo," NewMexicoHistory.org, http://newmexicohistory.org/people/ octaviano-ambrosio-larrazolo.
5. Ibid.
6. "John Moses," North Dakota State Historical Society, http://www. history.nd.gov/exhibits/governors/governors22.html.
7. George H.W. Bush, "Statement on the Appointment of Arnold Schwarzenegger as Chairman of the President's Council on Physical Fitness and Sports," January 22, 1990, http://www.presidency.ucsb. edu/ws/?pid=18049.
8. Arnold Schwarzenegger, "First Inaugural Address," January 17, 2003, http://governors.library.ca.gov/addresses/38-schwarzenegger01. html.

9. "James O Davidson," National Governors Association, https://www.nga.org/cms/home/governors/past-governors-bios/page_wisconsin/col2-content/main-content-list/title_davidson_james.default.html.

CHAPTER 5

1. Robert McFadden, "Vincent Impellitteri Is Dead," *New York Times*, January 30, 1987, http://www.nytimes.com/1987/01/30/obituaries/vincent-impellitteri-is-dead-mayor-of-new-york-in-1950-s.html?pagewanted=all.
2. Jerry Iannelli, "Hundreds Blast Gimenez, Demand Miami Remain Sanctuary City for Immigrants," *Miami New Times*, February 1, 2017, http://www.miaminewtimes.com/news/hundreds-blast-gimenez-demand-miami-remain-sanctuary-city-for-immigrants-9106729.

CHAPTER 6

1. Philip Bump, "Why Bernie Sanders Sees Henry Kissinger's Controversial History as an Asset," *Washington Post*, February 12, 2016, https://www.washingtonpost.com/news/the-fix/wp/2016/02/12/why-bernie-sanders-just-brought-up-hillary-clintons-ties-to-henry-kissinger/?utm_term=.4db5b514da6b.
2. "Henry Kissinger," Biography.com, http://www.biography.com/people/henry-kissinger-9366016#time-at-harvard.
3. Ron Grossman, "Henry Kissinger Recalls Military Service During World War II," *Chicago Tribune*, November 8, 2009, http://articles.chicagotribune.com/2009-11-08/news/0911070228_1_recalls-vietnam-war-military.
4. Robert K. Brigham, "Battlefield Vietnam: A Brief History," PBS.org, http://www.pbs.org/battlefieldvietnam/history/.
5. "Henry Kissinger," Biography.com, http://www.biography.com/people/henry-kissinger-9366016#washington-career.

6. Robert K. Brigham, "Battlefield Vietnam: A Brief History," PBS.org, http://www.pbs.org/battlefieldvietnam/history/.

7. Viet Thanh Nguyen, "Kissinger: The View from Vietnam," *The Atlantic*, November 27, 2016, https://www.theatlantic.com/international/archive/2016/11/kissinger-vietnam-nguyen/507851/.

8. "Madeleine Albright," Biography.com, http://www.biography.com/people/madeleine-albright-9179300#recent-years.

9. Ted Barrett, "Chao Confirmed as Transportation Secretary," CNN.com, January 31, 2017, http://www.cnn.com/2017/01/31/politics/elaine-chao-transportation-confirmation/.

10. "About OneAmerica," WeAreOneAmerica.org, http://weareoneamerica.org/about-oneamerica.

11. Arla Shephard, "Hate Free Zone Gets New Name, OneAmerica, With Justice for All," *Seattle Times*, June 30, 2008, http://www.seattletimes.com/seattle-news/hate-free-zone-gets-new-name-oneamerica-with-justice-for-all/.

12. "Jayapal Statement on President Trump's Muslim Ban 2.0," House.gov, March 7, 2017, https://jayapal.house.gov/media/press-releases/jayapal-statement-president-trump-s-muslim-ban-20.

GLOSSARY

ambassador A diplomat who is sent to a foreign country as a representative of his or her own country.

colony A region, typically under the rule of a distant country, occupied by settlers from that country.

constitution A document outlining the laws and rules by which a nation, state, or other entity is governed.

executive branch The branch of state or federal government responsible for enforcing the law.

famine An extreme food shortage that affects a large region or country, often leading residents to go hungry.

governor The head of the executive branch of government of a state.

Holocaust The term used to describe the Nazi-led genocide against Jews and other communities in Germany and Europe.

immigrant A person who moves to and resettles permanently in a foreign country.

judicial branch The branch of state or federal government responsible for interpreting the law.

justice A judge or magistrate.

legislative branch The branch of state or federal government that makes the law.

mayor In most American cities and towns, the head of local government.

politician A person who is officially involved in office or serving in an elected political position.

president The leader of the executive branch of government, which is an elected position in the United States.

sanctuary city A term used for American cities that are friendly to the needs of foreigners and immigrants, especially undocumented immigrants.

secretary of state In the United States, the person who leads the Department of State and handles the government's foreign affairs.

Supreme Court The highest court in the United States, in which nine sitting judges decide cases.

vice president The second-in-command of the executive branch of government in the United States.

Vietnam War Another name for the Second Indochina War, which ended in 1975 with the fall of Saigon.

FURTHER READING

BOOKS

Albright, Madeleine. *Madam Secretary: A Memoir.* New York, NY: Harper, 2013.

Hillard, Stephanie. *The US Capitol: The History of the US Congress.* New York, NY: KidsPower Press, 2017.

McAuliffe, Bill. *The US Supreme Court.* Mankato, MN: Creative Paperbacks, 2017.

Meyer, Susan Lynn. *Skating with the Statue of Liberty.* New York, NY: Yearling, 2017.

Mooney, Carla. *The Holocaust: Racism and Genocide in World War II.* White River Junction, VT: Nomad Press: 2017

Moss, Marissa. *Barbed Wire Baseball: How One Man Brought Hope to the Japanese Internment Camps of WWII.* New York, NY: Harry Abrams Books, 2016.

National Geographic. *Ellis Island.* Des Moines, IA: National Geographic Books, 2012.

Schwarzenegger, Arnold. *Total Recall: My Unbelievable True Life Story.* New York, NY: Simon and Schuster, 2012.

Sherman, Jill. *The Irish Potato Famine.* Minneapolis, MN: Lerner, 2016.

Vietnam War. New York, NY: DK Eyewitness Books, 2017.

WEBSITES

Ben's Guide to the US Government

bensguide.gpo.gov

Ben's Guide to the US Government is a service of the Government Publishing Office (GPO). It works to inform students, parents, and educators about the federal government and the way the government works.

Congress for Kids

congressforkids.net

Congress for Kids is a fun, interactive website designed for elementary and middle school students. It aims to help students learn about the three branches of government, especially the legislative branch.

Destination America

pbs.org/destinationamerica/usim.html

Destination America is an interactive learning module designed by the Public Broadcasting Service. It uses graphics and quizzes to help users understand the waves of immigration to the United States in the first decade of the twenty-first century.

Homeland: Immigration in America

pbs.org/program/homeland-immigration-america/

Homeland: Immigration in America is a documentary produced by the Public Broadcasting Service. It details the ways in which America has changed due to immigration from various parts of the world.

Immigration: Stories of Yesterday and Today

teacher.scholastic.com/activities/immigration/index.htm

Immigration: Stories of Yesterday and Today is a learning unit on immigration to the United States. Users can take a virtual field trip to Ellis Island and explore the experiences immigrants—past and present—had while making the journey to America.

INDEX

ABOUT THE AUTHOR

SUSAN NICHOLS

Susan Nichols has written several nonfiction books and biographies for young readers. She is interested in American and world history. She teaches English literature and lives in Baltimore, Maryland, with her family.